PEACH BOY

Library of Congress Cataloging-in-Publication Data

Sakurai, Gail.
    Peach Boy / by Gail Sakurai ; illustrated by Makiko Nagano.
      p.   cm. — (Legends of the world)
    Summary: When an old couple finds a baby inside a peach
floating on the river, they raise him as their son, and he grows up
to fight the terrible demons who have terrorized the village for years.
    ISBN 0-8167-3409-7 (library)   ISBN 0-8167-3410-0 (pbk.)
    [1. Folklore—Japan.]   I. Nagano, Makiko, ill. II. Title.
III. Series.
    PZ8.1.S2165Pe   1994
    398.2—dc20
    [E]   93-43178

LEGENDS OF THE WORLD

PEACH BOY

A JAPANESE LEGEND

RETOLD BY GAIL SAKURAI   ILLUSTRATED BY MAKIKO NAGANO

TROLL ASSOCIATES

A long time ago in Japan, there lived an old man and an old woman. They had a small but comfortable cottage in a village near the mountains. They both worked very hard to earn their living. The old man collected branches and sticks and sold them to the people in the village for firewood. The old woman did laundry for the villagers. The old couple was not poor, but they were sad and lonely because they had no children to brighten their days.

One day the old man went up to the mountains as usual to gather firewood. The old woman went down to the stream as usual to do the laundry. She was washing clothes on the bank of the stream when, suddenly, she heard an odd noise.

Swoosh-swish, plip-plop, swoosh-swish, plip-plop.

She looked up from her work. What was making that sound?

SWOOSH-SWISH, PLIP-PLOP, SWOOSH-SWISH, PLIP-PLOP.

The old woman could hardly believe her eyes. A giant peach was floating down the stream toward her! The peach bobbed close to her. She reached out her arms and grasped it, lifting it out of the water.

"Good gracious, it's so heavy!" she exclaimed. She decided to take the peach home as a special treat for her husband.

That evening when the old man returned from the mountains, the old woman showed him her prize. He was astonished when he saw the huge peach. When he heard the story of how the old woman had found it, he was flabbergasted.

"Let's get a knife and cut it open," he said. "I can hardly wait to taste it."

But just as they were about to slice into it, the peach wiggled.

"Did you see that?" the old man shouted. At that moment, the peach wiggled and jiggled.

"My goodness!" the old woman cried in surprise.

Just then the peach wiggled, and jiggled, and burst wide open. Out popped a baby boy!

The old folks decided that the boy must be a gift from heaven. They gave thanks that their prayers for a child had finally been answered. They named the baby Momotaro, which means Peach Boy.

The old mother and the old father took good care of Momotaro. He was the hungriest boy they had ever seen. If they gave him just one bowl of rice, he would eat it all and still be ready for more. If they gave him two bowls of rice, he would eat them both and still be ready for more. No matter how much food they gave him, he always ate it all and wanted more. Soon he grew big and strong. He was so strong that he could beat any of the village men at sword play and wrestling.

Momotaro helped his parents with their work. He carried the heavy bundles of wood for his father. He lifted the heavier baskets of laundry for his mother. The old people were happier than they had ever dreamed of being. At last they had a child to brighten their days.

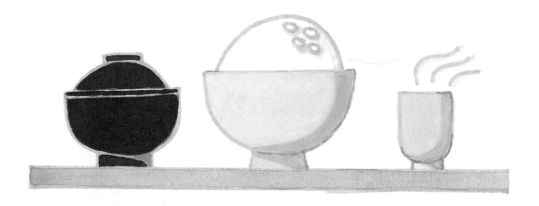

ow it happened that there were some terrible ogres who lived on an island in the western sea on the other side of the mountains. These ogres had been frightening the people in the villages, stealing their treasures, and breaking and damaging their property. Momotaro was as brave and kind as he was strong. He decided to go fight the ogres and make them stop terrifying the people.

When he told his parents about his plan, they were dismayed. They loved their son and did not want any harm to come to him. But he was determined, and nothing they said could change his mind. At last, they agreed to help him prepare for his adventure. The old man made him a banner and a sword. The old woman fixed his favorite dumplings and packed them in a pouch that he could carry at his waist.

Finally, it was time to say good-bye. The old folks stood in the doorway of the cottage and waved until Momotaro was out of sight.

Momotaro set off on his great adventure. He traveled through the high mountains. Soon he came upon a dog.

"Where are you going?" the dog asked.

"I am going to fight the terrible ogres," Momotaro answered.

"Mmm . . . those dumplings smell delicious. If you share them with me, I will come with you and help you fight the ogres," the dog said.

"Very well," replied Momotaro, and he gave the dog a dumpling.

The two companions set off together on their great adventure. They traveled through the high mountains. Soon they came upon a monkey.

"Where are you going?" the monkey asked.

"We are going to fight the terrible ogres," Momotaro answered.

"Mmm . . . those dumplings smell delicious. If you share them with me, I will come with you and help you fight the ogres," the monkey said.

"Very well," replied Momotaro, and he gave the monkey a dumpling.

The three companions set off together through the high mountains. Soon they came upon a pheasant.

"Where are you going?" the pheasant asked.

"We are going to fight the terrible ogres," Momotaro answered.

"Mmm . . . those dumplings smell delicious. If you share them with me, I will come with you and help you fight the ogres," the pheasant said.

"Very well," replied Momotaro, and he gave the pheasant a dumpling.

The four companions set off together on their great adventure. They traveled through the high mountains.

Finally, they reached the shore of the western sea. In the distance they could see the island where the terrible ogres lived.

They climbed into the boat that was waiting on the shore and rowed out to the ogres' island.

When they landed, they marched up to the ogres'
castle and pounded on the heavy wooden gate.

"Who is there?" shouted the chief ogre.

"It is I, Momotaro. I have come to fight you and take
back all the treasures you have stolen from the people."

The ogres laughed loudly at that and refused to open
the gate. Momotaro and his companions put their heads
together and made a plan to get into the castle.

22

The pheasant flew over the wall and started attacking the ogres. He swooped down and pecked at them with his beak and raked them with his claws. While the ogres were distracted by the pheasant's attacks, the monkey climbed over the wall and opened the heavy gate from the inside. Then Momotaro and the dog dashed inside and joined the fight against the ogres.

The monkey climbed on the ogres and scratched them. The dog snarled and bit their arms and legs. Momotaro rushed in and fearlessly swung at the ogres with his sword. He knocked the ogres down and then picked them up one by one, spun them around and around, and tossed them into a pile on the ground. He was so strong that the ogres were no match for him. Soon he had defeated them all.

"We surrender, Momotaro," they sobbed. "We will do whatever you say."

"You must return all the treasures you stole and promise never to bother the village people again," Momotaro commanded.

"We promise, oh great warrior," the ogres cried.

omotaro and his companions gathered up all the stolen treasures and loaded them into a cart. Then they returned home by the same route, pulling the cart behind them.

When they finally arrived at Momotaro's village, they were greeted by cheering crowds. Momotaro's parents were so relieved to see their son unharmed, and so proud of his courage, that they wept with joy. All the treasures were returned to their rightful owners. Momotaro and his three companions happily went home to the little cottage with the old mother and the old father. They all lived together there in peace and contentment until the end of their days.

The legend of *Peach Boy* is one of Japan's best-known folktales. Japan is located along the eastern coast of Asia. It consists of a group of mountainous islands: four main ones (Hokkaido, Honshu, Shikoku, and Kyushu) and thousands of smaller ones. With its forested mountains and rich, fertile lowlands, ancient Japan was primarily agricultural. Farmers grew crops such as millet (which was used in Momotaro's dumplings) and rice.

The Japanese hold national festivals in honor of their children. One of these is the Iris Festival *(Shobu-no-sekku)*. The long blades of the iris are symbolic of the sword, which is the soul of the Samurai warrior. This festival was once known as Boys' Day but is now called Children's Day. Families display various dolls that represent cultural heroes. The dolls are meant to encourage *Bushido*, a strict code of honor, chivalry, and devotion. These qualities were all present in Momotaro.

The Festival of the Peach *(Momo-no-sekku)* honors the peach blossom, which symbolizes grace and gentleness. This festival coincides with the Doll Festival, or Girls' Day. Japanese mothers display dolls that represent the imperial household. These dolls are handed down from generation to generation. Mothers use them to teach their daughters the value of loyalty, devotion, and pride in their heritage.